⫷ **W9-BYE-942**

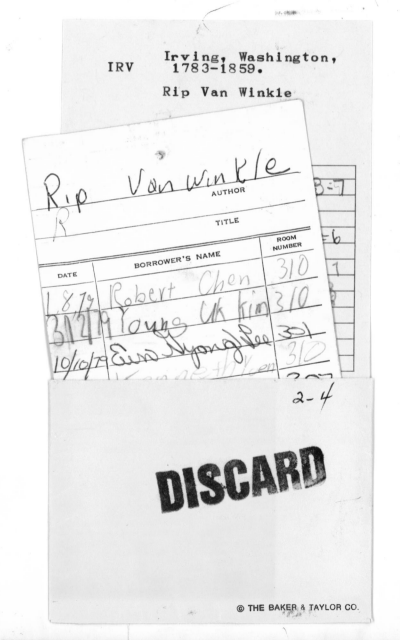

IRV   Irving, Washington,
         1783-1859.

     Rip Van Winkle

Rip Van Winkle

AUTHOR

TITLE

DATE	BORROWER'S NAME	ROOM NUMBER
1/8/79	Robert Chen	310
3/2/79	Young Uk Kim	310
10/10/79	Eun Hyong Lee	301
	Kenneth Yeen	310

2-4

DISCARD

© THE BAKER & TAYLOR CO.

RIP VAN WINKLE

IRV
C1

WASHINGTON IRVING

RIP VAN WINKLE

PEIRCE SCHOOL
1423 BRYN MAWR AVE.
CHICAGO, ILLINOIS 60626

WITH DRAWINGS BY

ARTHUR RACKHAM

J. B. LIPPINCOTT COMPANY

PHILADELPHIA AND NEW YORK

Library of Congress Catalog Card Number 67–19272

Printed in Great Britain

CONTENTS

LIST OF ILLUSTRATIONS

vii

LIST OF ILLUSTRATIONS

By Woden, God of Saxons,

From whence comes Wensday, that is Wodensday,

Truth is a thing that ever I will keep

Unto thylke day in which I creep into

My sepulchre—

CARTWRIGHT

INTRODUCTION

The following Tale was found among
the papers of the late Diedrich Knick-
erbocker, an old gentleman of New
York, who was very curious in the
Dutch history of the province, and the
manners of the descendants from its
primitive settlers. His historical researches, however, did not lie so much
among books as among men; for the

former are lamentably scanty on his favourite topics; whereas he found the old burghers, and still more their wives, rich in that legendary lore so invaluable to true history. Whenever, therefore, he happened upon a genuine Dutch family, snugly shut up in its low-roofed farmhouse, under a spreading sycamore, he looked upon it as a little clasped volume of black-letter, and studied it with the zeal of a bookworm.

The result of all these researches was a history of the province during the reign of the Dutch governors, which he published some years since. There have been various opinions as to the literary character of his work, and, to tell the truth, it is not a whit better than it should be. Its chief merit is its scrupulous accuracy, which indeed was a little questioned on its first appearance, but has since been completely established; and it is now admitted into all historical collections as a book of unquestionable authority.

The old gentleman died shortly after the publication of his work; and now that he is dead and gone, it cannot do much harm to his memory to say that his time might have been much better employed in weightier labours. He, however, was apt to ride his hobby his own way; and though it did now and then kick up the dust a little in the eyes of his neighbours, and grieve the spirit of some friends, for whom he felt the truest deference and affection, yet his errors and follies are remembered "more in sorrow than in anger," and it begins to be suspected that he never intended to injure or offend. But however his memory may be appreciated by critics, it is still held dear by many folks whose good opinion is well worth having; particularly by certain biscuit-bakers, who have gone so far as to imprint his likeness on their New-Year cakes; and have thus given him a chance for immortality, almost equal to the being stamped on a Waterloo Medal, or a Queen Anne's Farthing.

RIP VAN WINKLE

OEVER has made a voyage up the Hudson must remember the Kaatskill Mountains. They are a dismembered branch of the great Appalachian family, and are seen away to the west of the river, swelling up to a noble height, and lording it over the surrounding country. Every change of season, every change of weather, indeed, every hour of the day, produces some change in the magical hues and shapes of these mountains, and they are regarded by all the good wives, far and near, as perfect barometers. When the weather is fair and settled, they are clothed in blue and purple, and print their bold outlines on the clear evening sky; but sometimes, when the rest of the landscape is cloudless, they will gather a hood of grey vapours about their summits, which, in the last rays of the setting sun, will glow and light up like a crown of glory.

At the foot of these fairy mountains, the voyager may have descried the light smoke curling up from a village, whose

2

shingle-roofs gleam among the trees, just where the blue tints of the upland melt away into the fresh green of the nearer landscape. It is a little village, of great antiquity, having been founded by some of the Dutch colonists in the early times of the province, just about the beginning of the government of the good Peter Stuyvesant (may he rest in peace!), and there were some of the houses of the original settlers standing within a few years, built of small yellow bricks brought from Holland, having latticed windows and gable fronts, surmounted with weathercocks.

In that same village, and in one of these very houses (which, to tell the precise truth, was sadly time-worn and weather-beaten), there lived, many years since, while the country was yet a province of Great Britain, a simple, good-natured fellow, of the name of Rip Van Winkle. He was a descendant of the Van Winkles who figured so gallantly in the chivalrous days of Peter Stuyvesant, and accompanied him to the siege of Port Christina. He inherited, however, but little of the martial character of his ancestors. I have observed that he was a simple, good-natured man; he was, moreover, a kind neighbour, and an obedient, hen-pecked husband. Indeed, to the latter circumstance might be owing that meekness of spirit which gained him such universal popularity; for those men are most apt to be obsequious and conciliating abroad, who are under the discipline of shrews at home. Their tempers, doubtless, are rendered pliant and malleable in the fiery furnace of domestic tribulation; and a curtain-lecture is worth all the sermons in the world for teaching the virtues of patience and long-suffering. A termagant wife may, therefore, in some respects, be considered a tolerable blessing; and if so, Rip Van Winkle was thrice blessed.

Certain it is, that he was a great favourite among all the good wives of the village, who, as usual with the amiable sex, took his part in all family squabbles; and never failed, whenever they talked those matters over in their evening gossipings, to lay all the blame on Dame Van Winkle. The children of the village, too, would shout with joy whenever he approached. He assisted at their sports, made their playthings, taught them to fly kites and shoot marbles, and told them long stories of ghosts, witches, and Indians. Whenever he went dodging about the village, he was surrounded by a troop of them, hanging on his skirts, clambering on his back, and playing a thousand tricks on him with impunity; and not a dog would bark at him throughout the neighbourhood.

The great error in Rip's composition was an insuperable aversion to all kinds of profitable labour. It could not be from the want of assiduity or persever-ance; for he would sit on a wet rock, with a rod as long and heavy as a Tartar's lance, and fish all day without a murmur, even though he should not be encouraged by a single nibble. He would carry a fowling-piece on his shoulder for hours together, trudging through woods and swamps, and up hill and down dale, to shoot a few squirrels or wild pigeons. He would never refuse to assist a neighbour even in the roughest toil, and was a foremost man at all country frolics for husking Indian corn, or building stone fences; the women of the village, too, used to employ him to run their errands, and to do such little odd jobs as their less obliging husbands would not do for them. In a word, Rip was ready to attend to anybody's business but his own; but as to doing family duty, and keeping his farm in order, he found it impossible.

In fact, he declared it was of no use to work on his farm; it was the most pestilent little piece of ground in the whole country; everything about it went wrong, and would go wrong,

8

These fairy mountains

His likeness on their New-Year cakes

Regarded by all the good wives . . . as perfect barometers

A curtain-lecture is worth all the sermons in the world

in spite of him. His fences were con-
tinually falling to pieces; his cow
would either go astray, or get among
the cabbages; weeds were sure to grow
quicker in his fields than anywhere
else; the rain always made a point of
setting in just as he had some outdoor
work to do; so that though his pat-
rimonial estate had dwindled
under his management acre by acre,
until there was little more left than a
mere patch of Indian corn and pota-
toes, yet it was the worst conditioned
farm in the neighbourhood.

His children, too, were as ragged
and wild as if they belonged to nobody. His son Rip, an urchin begotten

in his own likeness, promised to inherit the habits, with the old clothes, of his father. He was generally seen trooping like a colt at his mother's heels, equipped in a pair of his father's cast-off galligaskins, which he had much ado to hold up with one hand, as a fine lady does her train in bad weather.

Rip Van Winkle, however, was one of those happy mortals, of foolish, well-oiled dispositions, who take the world easy, eat white bread or brown, whichever can be got with the least thought or trouble, and would rather starve on a penny than work for a pound. If left to himself, he would have whistled life away in perfect

contentment; but his wife kept con-
tinually dinning in his ears about his
idleness, his carelessness, and the ruin
he was bringing on his family. Morning,
noon, and night, her tongue was incessantly going, and everything he said
or did was sure to produce a torrent
of household eloquence. Rip had but
one way of replying to all lectures of
the kind, and that, by frequent use, had
grown into a habit. He shrugged his
shoulders, shook his head, cast up his
eyes, but said nothing. This, however,
always provoked a fresh volley from
his wife; so that he was fain to draw
off his forces, and take to the outside
of the house—the only side which, in

truth, belongs to a hen-pecked husband.

Rip's sole domestic adherent was his dog Wolf, who was as much hen-pecked as his master; for Dame Van Winkle regarded them as companions in idleness, and even looked upon Wolf with an evil eye, as the cause of his master's going so often astray. True it is, in all points of spirit befitting an honourable dog, he was as courageous an animal as ever scoured the woods; but what courage can withstand the ever-during and all-besetting terrors of a woman's tongue? The moment Wolf entered the house his crest fell, his tail drooped to the ground, or curled between his legs, he sneaked about with a gallows air, casting many a sidelong glance at Dame Van Winkle, and at the least flourish of a broomstick or ladle he would fly to the door with yelping precipitation.

Times grew worse and worse with Rip Van Winkle as years of matrimony rolled on; a tart temper never mellows with age, and a sharp tongue is the only edged tool that grows keener with constant use. For a long while he used to console himself, when driven from home, by frequenting a kind of perpetual club of the sages, philosophers, and other idle personages of the village, which held its sessions on a bench before a small inn, designated by a rubicund portrait of His Majesty George the Third. Here they used to sit in the shade through a long, lazy summer's day, talking listlessly over village gossip, or telling endless sleepy stories about nothing. But it would have been worth any statesman's money to have heard the profound discussions that sometimes took place, when by chance an old newspaper fell into their hands from some passing traveller. How solemnly they would listen to the contents, as drawled out by Derrick Van Bummel, the schoolmaster, a dapper, learned little man, who was not to be daunted by the

most gigantic word in the dictionary;
and how sagely they would deliberate
upon public events some months after
they had taken place.

The opinions of this junto were
completely controlled by Nicholas
Vedder, a patriarch of the village, and
landlord of the inn, at the door of
which he took his seat from morning
till night, just moving sufficiently to
avoid the sun and keep in the shade
of a large tree; so that the neighbours
could tell the hour by his movements
as accurately as by a sun-dial. It is
true he was rarely heard to speak, but
smoked his pipe incessantly. His adherents, however (for every great man

has his adherents), perfectly understood him, and knew how to gather his opinions. When anything that was read or related displeased him, he was observed to smoke his pipe vehemently, and to send forth short, frequent, and angry puffs; but when pleased, he would inhale the smoke slowly and tranquilly, and emit it in light and placid clouds; and sometimes, taking the pipe from his mouth, and letting the fragrant vapour curl about his nose, would gravely nod his head in token of perfect approbation.

From even this stronghold the un-lucky Rip was at length routed by his termagant wife, who would suddenly

break in upon the tranquillity of the
assemblage and call the members all to
naught; nor was that august personage,
Nicholas Vedder himself, sacred from
the daring tongue of this terrible
virago, who charged him outright with
encouraging her husband in habits of
idleness.

Poor Rip was at last reduced almost
to despair; and his only alternative, to
escape from the labour of the farm and
clamour of his wife, was to take gun
in hand and stroll away into the woods.
Here he would sometimes seat himself
at the foot of a tree, and share the
contents of his wallet with Wolf, with
whom he sympathised as a fellow

sufferer in persecution. "Poor Wolf,"
he would say, "thy mistress leads thee
a dog's life of it; but never mind, my
lad, whilst I live thou shalt never want
a friend to stand by thee!" Wolf would
wag his tail, look wistfully in his
master's face; and, if dogs can feel pity,
I verily believe he reciprocated the
sentiment with all his heart.

In a long ramble of the kind on a
fine autumnal day, Rip had uncon-
sciously scrambled to one of the highest parts of the Kaatskill Mountains.
He was after his favourite sport of
squirrel shooting, and the still solitudes
had echoed and re-echoed with the
reports of his gun. Panting and

fatigued, he threw himself, late in the afternoon, on a green knoll, covered with mountain herbage, that crowned the brow of a precipice. From an opening between the trees he could overlook all the lower country for many a mile of rich woodland. He saw at a distance the lordly Hudson, far, far below him, moving on its silent but majestic course, with the reflection of a purple cloud, or the sail of a lagging bark, here and there sleeping on its glassy bosom, and at last losing itself in the blue highlands.

On the other side he looked down into a deep mountain glen, wild, lonely, and shagged, the bottom filled with fragments from the impending cliffs, and scarcely lighted by the reflected rays of the setting sun. For some time Rip lay musing on this scene; evening was gradually advancing; the mountains began to throw their long blue shadows over the valleys; he saw that it would be dark long before he could reach the village, and he heaved a heavy sigh when he thought of encountering the terrors of Dame Van Winkle.

As he was about to descend, he heard a voice from a distance, hallooing, "Rip Van Winkle! Rip Van Winkle!" He looked round, but could see nothing but a crow winging its

solitary flight across the mountain. He
thought his fancy must have deceived
him, and turned again to descend,
when he heard the same cry ring
through the still evening air: "Rip
Van Winkle! Rip Van Winkle!" At
the same time Wolf bristled up his
back, and giving a low growl, skulked
to his master's side, looking fearfully
down into the glen. Rip now felt a
vague apprehension stealing over him;
he looked anxiously in the same
direction, and perceived a strange figure
slowly toiling up the rocks, and bend-
ing under the weight of something he
carried on his back. He was surprised
to see any human being in this lonely

and unfrequented place; but supposing it to be some one of the neighbourhood in need of his assistance, he hastened down to yield it.

On nearer approach he was still more surprised at the singularity of the stranger's appearance. He was a short, square-built old fellow, with thick bushy hair, and a grizzled beard. His dress was of the antique Dutch fashion, —a cloth jerkin strapped round the waist—several pair of breeches, the outer one of ample volume, decorated with rows of buttons down the sides, and punches at the knees. He bore on his shoulder a stout keg, that seemed full of liquor, and made signs for Rip to approach and assist him with the load. Though rather shy and distrustful of his new acquaintance, Rip complied with his usual alacrity; and mutually relieving one another, they clambered up a narrow gully, apparently the dry bed of a mountain torrent. As they ascended, Rip every now and then heard long, rolling peals, like distant thunder, that seemed to issue out of a deep ravine, or rather cleft, between lofty rocks, towards which their ragged path conducted. He paused for an instant, but supposing it to be the muttering of one of those transient thunder-showers which often take place in mountain heights, he proceeded.

Passing through the ravine, they came to a hollow, like a small amphitheatre, surrounded by perpendicular precipices, over the brinks of which impending trees shot their branches, so that you only caught glimpses of the azure sky and the bright evening cloud. During the whole time Rip and his companion had laboured on in silence; for though the former marvelled greatly what could be the object of carrying a keg of liquor up this wild mountain, yet there was something strange and incomprehensible about the unknown that inspired awe and checked familiarity.

On entering the amphitheatre, new objects of wonder presented themselves.

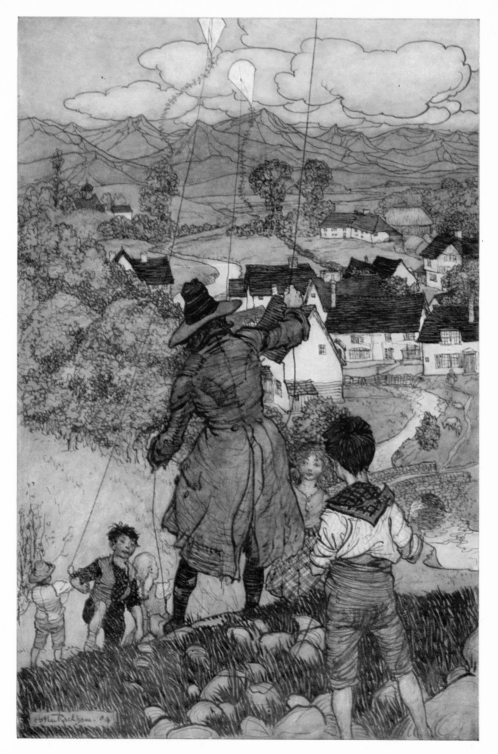

Taught them to fly kites

His children were as ragged and wild as if they belonged to nobody

They clambered up a narrow gully

His heart turned within him, and his knees smote together

On a level spot in the centre was a
company of odd-looking personages
playing at nine-pins. They were dressed
in a quaint, outlandish fashion; some
wore short doublets, others jerkins, with
long knives in their belts, and most of
them had enormous breeches of similar
style with that of the guide's. Their
visages, too, were peculiar: one had a
large beard, broad face, and small
piggish eyes; the face of another seemed
to consist entirely of nose, and was surmounted by a white sugar-loaf hat set
off with a little red cock's tail. They
all had beards, of various shapes and
colours. There was one who seemed
to be the commander. He was a stout

old gentleman, with a weather-beaten
countenance; he wore a laced doublet,
broad belt and hanger, high-crowned
hat and feather, red stockings, and high-
heeled shoes with roses in them. The
whole group reminded Rip of the
figures in an old Flemish painting, in
the parlour of Dominie Van Shaick,
the village parson, and which had been
brought over from Holland at the time
of the settlement.

What seemed particularly odd to
Rip was, that, though these folks were
evidently amusing themselves, yet they
maintained the gravest faces, the most
mysterious silence, and were, withal,
the most melancholy party of pleasure

he had ever witnessed. Nothing inter-
rupted the stillness of the scene but the
noise of the balls, which, whenever
they were rolled, echoed along the
mountains like rumbling peals of
thunder.

As Rip and his companion approached them, they suddenly desisted
from their play, and stared at him with
such fixed, statue-like gaze, and such
strange, uncouth, lack-lustre counten-
ances, that his heart turned within him,
and his knees smote together. His
companion now emptied the contents
of the keg into large flagons, and made
signs to him to wait upon the company. He obeyed with fear and trem-

bling; they quaffed the liquor in profound silence, and then returned to their game.

By degrees Rip's awe and apprehension subsided. He even ventured, when no eye was fixed upon him, to taste the beverage, which he found had much of the flavour of excellent Hollands. He was naturally a thirsty soul, and was soon tempted to repeat the draught. One taste provoked another; and he reiterated his visits to the flagon so often that at length his senses were overpowered, his eyes swam in his head, his head gradually declined, and he fell into a deep sleep.

On waking, he found himself on the

green knoll whence he had first seen
the old man of the glen. He rubbed
his eyes—it was a bright sunny morning. The birds were hopping and
twittering among the bushes, and the
eagle was wheeling aloft and breasting
the pure mountain breeze. "Surely,"
thought Rip, "I have not slept here all
night." He recalled the occurrences
before he fell asleep. The strange man
with a keg of liquor—the mountain
ravine—the wild retreat among the
rocks—the woe-begone party at nine-
pins—the flagon—"Oh! that flagon!
that wicked flagon!" thought Rip—
"What excuse shall I make to Dame
Van Winkle?"

He looked round for his gun, but in place of the clean, well-oiled fowling-piece, he found an old firelock lying by him, the barrel incrusted with rust, the lock falling off, and the stock worm-eaten. He now suspected that the grave roysterers of the mountain had put a trick upon him, and, having dosed him with liquor, had robbed him of his gun. Wolf, too, had disappeared, but he might have strayed away after a squirrel or partridge. He whistled after him, and shouted his name, but all in vain; the echoes repeated his whistle and shout, but no dog was to be seen.

He determined to revisit the scene

of the last evening's gambol, and if he
met with any of the party, to demand
his dog and gun. As he rose to walk,
he found himself stiff in the joints, and
wanting in his usual activity. "These
mountain beds do not agree with me,"
thought Rip, "and if this frolic should
lay me up with a fit of the rheumatism,
I shall have a blessed time with Dame
Van Winkle." With some difficulty
he got down into the glen: he found
the gully up which he and his companion had ascended the preceding
evening; but to his astonishment a
mountain stream was now foaming
down it, leaping from rock to rock,
and filling the glen with babbling

murmurs. He, however, made shift to scramble up its sides, working his toilsome way through thickets of birch, sassafras, and witch-hazel, and sometimes tripped up or entangled by the wild grape-vines that twisted their coils or tendrils from tree to tree, and spread a kind of network in his path.

At length he reached to where the ravine had opened through the cliffs to the amphitheatre; but no traces of such opening remained. The rocks presented a high, impenetrable wall, over which the torrent came tumbling in a sheet of feathery foam, and fell into a broad deep basin, black from the shadows of the surrounding forest.

Here, then, poor Rip was brought to a
stand. He again called and whistled
after his dog; he was only answered by
the cawing of a flock of idle crows,
sporting high in air about a dry tree
that overhung a sunny precipice; and
who, secure in their elevation, seemed
to look down and scoff at the poor
man's perplexities. What was to be
done? the morning was passing away,
and Rip felt famished for want of his
breakfast. He grieved to give up his
dog and gun; he dreaded to meet his
wife; but it would not do to starve
among the mountains. He shook his
head, shouldered the rusty firelock,
and, with a heart full of trouble and

anxiety, turned his steps homeward.

As he approached the village he met a number of people, but none whom he knew, which somewhat surprised him, for he had thought himself acquainted with every one in the country round. Their dress, too, was of a different fashion from that to which he was accustomed. They all stared at him with equal marks of surprise, and whenever they cast their eyes upon him, invariably stroked their chins. The constant recurrence of this gesture induced Rip, involuntarily, to do the same, when, to his astonishment, he found his beard had grown a foot long!

He had now entered the skirts of

the village. A troop of strange children
ran at his heels, hooting after him, and
pointing at his grey beard. The dogs,
too, not one of which he recognised for
an old acquaintance, barked at him as
he passed. The very village was altered;
it was larger and more populous. There
were rows of houses which he had never
seen before, and those which had been
his familiar haunts had disappeared.
Strange names were over the doors—
strange faces at the windows—everything was strange. His mind now mis-
gave him; he began to doubt whether
both he and the world around him were
not bewitched. Surely this was his
native village, which he had left but the

35

day before. There stood the Kaatskill Mountains—there ran the silver Hudson at a distance—there was every hill and dale precisely as it had always been. Rip was sorely perplexed. "That flagon last night," thought he, "has addled my poor head sadly!"

It was with some difficulty that he found the way to his own house, which he approached with silent awe, expecting every moment to hear the shrill voice of Dame Van Winkle. He found the house gone to decay—the roof fallen in, the windows shattered, and the doors off the hinges. A half-starved dog that looked like Wolf was skulking about it. Rip called him

by name, but the cur snarled, showed
his teeth, and passed on. This was an
unkind cut indeed. "My very dog,"
sighed poor Rip, "has forgotten me!"

He entered the house, which, to tell
the truth, Dame Van Winkle had
always kept in neat order. It was empty,
forlorn, and apparently abandoned. This
desolateness overcame all his connubial
fears—he called loudly for his wife and
children—the lonely chambers rang for
a moment with his voice, and then all
again was silence.

He now hurried forth and hastened
to his old resort, the village inn—but
it too was gone. A large rickety wood-
en building stood in its place, with great

37

gaping windows, some of them broken and mended with old hats and petticoats, and over the door was painted, "The Union Hotel, by Jonathan Doolittle." Instead of the great tree that used to shelter the quiet little Dutch inn of yore, there was now reared a tall, naked pole, with something on the top that looked like a red nightcap, and from it was fluttering a flag, on which was a singular assemblage of stars and stripes; all this was strange and incomprehensible. He recognised on the sign, however, the ruby face of King George, under which he had smoked so many a peaceful pipe; but even this was singularly metamorphosed. The red coat was changed for one of blue and buff, a sword was held in the hand instead of a sceptre, the head was decorated with a cocked hat, and underneath was painted in large characters, GENERAL WASHINGTON.

There was, as usual, a crowd of folk about the door, but none that Rip recollected. The very character of the people seemed changed. There was a busy, bustling, disputatious tone about it, instead of the accustomed phlegm and drowsy tranquillity. He looked in vain for the sage Nicholas Vedder, with his broad face, double chin, and fair long pipe, uttering clouds of tobacco-smoke instead of idle speeches; or Van

Bummel, the schoolmaster, doling forth the contents of an ancient newspaper. In place of these, a lean, bilious-looking fellow, with his pockets full of handbills, was haranguing vehemently about rights of citizens—elections—members of congress—liberty—Bunker's Hill— heroes of seventy-six—and other words, which were a perfect Babylonish jargon to the bewildered Van Winkle.

The appearance of Rip, with his long, grizzled beard, his rusty fowling-piece, his uncouth dress and an army of women and children at his heels, soon attracted the attention of the tavern-politicians. They crowded round him, eyeing him from head to foot with

He even ventured . . . to taste the beverage

He fell into a deep sleep

The cawing of a flock of idle crows

A troop of strange children ran at his heels

great curiosity. The orator bustled up
to him, and, drawing him partly aside,
inquired on which side he voted.
Rip stared in vacant stupidity. Another short but busy little fellow pulled
him by the arm, and, rising on tiptoe,
inquired in his ear whether he was
Federal or Democrat. Rip was equally
at a loss to comprehend the question;
when a knowing, self-important old
gentleman, in a sharp cocked hat,
made his way through the crowd,
putting them to the right and left with
his elbows as he passed, and planting
himself before Van Winkle, with one
arm akimbo, the other resting on his
cane, his keen eyes and sharp hat pen-

etrating, as it were, into his very soul,
demanded in an austere tone what
brought him to the election with a
gun on his shoulder, and a mob at his
heels; and whether he meant to breed
a riot in the village.

"Alas! gentlemen," cried Rip, somewhat dismayed, "I am a poor quiet
man, a native of the place, and a loyal
subject of the King, God bless him!"

Here a general shout burst from the
bystanders—"A tory! a tory! a spy! a
refugee! hustle him! away with him!"
It was with great difficulty that the self-
important man in the cocked hat re-
stored order; and, having assumed a
tenfold austerity of brow, demanded

again of the unknown culprit, what he came there for, and whom he was seeking. The poor man humbly assured him that he meant no harm, but merely came there in search of some of his neighbours, who used to keep about the tavern.

"Well — who are they? — name them."

Rip bethought himself a moment, and inquired, "Whére's Nicholas Vedder?"

There was a silence for a little while, when an old man replied, in a thin, piping voice, "Nicholas Vedder! why, he is dead and gone these eighteen years! There was a wooden tombstone in the churchyard that used to tell all about him, but that's rotten and gone too."

"Where's Brom Dutcher?"

"Oh, he went off to the army in the beginning of the war; some say he was killed at the storming of Stony Point— others say he was drowned in a squall at the foot of Antony's Nose. I don't know—he never came back again."

"Where's Van Bummel, the school-master?"

"He went off to the wars too, was a great militia general, and is now in congress."

Rip's heart died away at hearing of these sad changes in his home and friends, and finding himself thus alone in the world. Every answer puzzled him too, by treating of such enormous lapses of time, and of matters which he could not understand: war—congress—Stony Point,—he had no courage to ask after any more friends, but cried out in despair, "Does nobody here know Rip Van Winkle?"

"Oh, Rip Van Winkle!" exclaimed two or three, "oh, to be sure! that's Rip Van Winkle yonder, leaning against the tree."

Rip looked, and beheld a precise counterpart of himself, as he went up the mountain; apparently as lazy, and certainly as ragged. The poor fellow was now completely confounded. He doubted his own identity, and whether he was himself or another man. In the midst of his bewilderment, the man in the cocked hat demanded who he was, and what was his name.

"God knows," exclaimed he, at his wit's end; "I'm not myself—I'm somebody else—that's me yonder—no—that's somebody else got into my shoes—I was myself last night, but I fell asleep on the mountain, and they've changed my gun, and everything's changed, and I'm changed, and I can't tell what's my name, or who I am!"

The bystanders began now to look at each other, nod, wink significantly,

and tap their fingers against their fore-
heads. There was a whisper, also, about
securing the gun, and keeping the old
fellow from doing mischief, at the very
suggestion of which the self-important
man in the cocked hat retired with some
precipitation. At this critical moment
a fresh, comely woman pressed through
the throng to get a peep at the grey-
bearded man. She had a chubby child
in her arms, which, frightened at his
looks, began to cry. "Hush, Rip,"
cried she, "hush, you little fool; the
old man won't hurt you." The name
of the child, the air of the mother, the
tone of her voice, all awakened a train
of recollections in his mind. "What

47

is your name, my good woman?"
asked he.

"Judith Gardenier."

"And your father's name?"

"Ah, poor man, Rip Van Winkle
was his name, but it's twenty years since
he went away from home with his gun,
and never has been heard of since—his
dog came home without him; but
whether he shot himself, or was carried
away by the Indians, nobody can tell.
I was then but a little girl."

Rip had but one question more to
ask; but he put it with a faltering voice:

"Where's your mother?"

"Oh, she too has died but a short
time since; she broke a blood-vessel

in a fit of passion at a New-England
pedlar."

There was a drop of comfort, at
least, in this intelligence. The honest
man could contain himself no longer.
He caught his daughter and her child
in his arms. "I am your father!" cried
he—"Young Rip Van Winkle once—
old Rip Van Winkle now!—Does nobody know poor Rip Van Winkle?"

All stood amazed, until an old woman,
tottering out from among the crowd,
put her hand to her brow, and peering
under it in his face for a moment, exclaimed, "Sure enough! it is Rip Van
Winkle—it is himself! Welcome home
again, old neighbour. Why, where

have you been these twenty long years?"

Rip's story was soon told, for the whole twenty years had been to him but as one night. The neighbours stared when they heard it; some were seen to wink at each other, and put their tongues in their cheeks; and the self-important man in the cocked hat, who, when the alarm was over, had returned to the field, screwed down the corners of his mouth, and shook his head—upon which there was a general shaking of the head throughout the assemblage.

It was determined, however, to take the opinion of old Peter Vanderdonk, who was seen slowly advancing up the road. He was a descendant of the historian of that name, who wrote one of the earliest accounts of the province. Peter was the most ancient inhabitant of the village, and well versed in all the wonderful events and traditions of the neighbourhood. He recollected Rip at once, and corroborated his story in the most satisfactory manner. He assured the company that it was a fact, handed down from his ancestor the historian, that the Kaatskill Mountains had always been haunted by strange beings. That it was affirmed that the great Hendrick Hudson, the first discoverer of the river and country, kept a kind of vigil there every twenty years, with his crew of the *Half Moon*; being permitted in this way to revisit the scenes of his enterprise, and keep a guardian eye upon the river and the great city called by his name. That his father had once seen them in their old Dutch dresses playing at nine-pins in a hollow of the mountain; and that he himself had heard, one summer afternoon, the sound of their balls, like distant peals of thunder.

To make a long story short, the company broke up and returned to the more important concerns of the election. Rip's daughter took him home to live with her; she had a snug, well-furnished house, and a stout, cheery farmer for a husband, whom Rip recollected for one of the urchins that used to climb upon his back. As to Rip's son and heir, who was the ditto of himself, seen leaning against the tree, he was employed to work on the farm; but evinced an hereditary disposition to attend to anything else but his business.

Rip now resumed his old walks and habits; he soon found many of his former cronies, though all rather the worse for the wear and tear of time; and preferred making friends among the rising generation, with whom he soon grew into great favour.

Having nothing to do at home, and being arrived at that happy age when a man can be idle with impunity, he took his place once more on the bench at the inn-door, and was reverenced as one of the patriarchs of the village, and a chronicler of the old times "before the war." It was some time before he could get into the regular track of gossip, or could be made to comprehend the strange events that had taken place during his torpor. How that there had been a revolutionary war; that the country had thrown off the yoke of old England, and that, instead of being a subject of His Majesty George the Third, he was now a free citizen of the United States. Rip, in fact, was no politician; the changes of states and empires made but little impression on him; but there was one species of despotism under which he had long groaned, and that was—petticoat government. Happily that was at an end; he had got his neck out of the yoke of matrimony, and could go in and out whenever he pleased, without dreading the tyranny of Dame Van Winkle. Whenever her name was mentioned, however, he shook his head, shrugged his shoulders, and cast up his eyes; which might pass either for an expression of resignation to his fate, or joy at his deliverance.

He used to tell his story to every stranger that arrived at Mr. Doolittle's hotel. He was observed, at first, to vary on some points every time he told it, which was, doubtless, owing to his having so recently awaked. It at last settled down precisely to the tale I have related, and not a man, woman, or child in the neighbourhood but knew it by heart. Some always pretended to doubt the reality of it, and insisted that Rip had been out of his head, and that this was one point on which he always remained flighty. The old Dutch inhabitants, however, almost universally gave it full credit. Even to this day they never hear a thunder-storm of a summer afternoon about the Kaatskill, but they say Hendrick Hudson and his crew are at their game of nine-pins;

The dogs . . . barked at him as he passed

The most ancient inhabitant of the village

He . . . preferred making friends among the rising generation

They never hear a thunder-storm . . . but they say Hendrick Hudson
and his crew are at their game of nine-pins

and it is a common wish of all hen-
pecked husbands in the neighbourhood,
when life hangs heavy on their hands,
that they might have a quieting draught
out of Rip Van Winkle's flagon.

POSTSCRIPT

The following are travelling notes from a memorandum book of Mr. Knicker-bocker.

The Kaatsberg or Catskill Mountains have always been a region full of fable.

POSTSCRIPT

The Indians considered them the abode of spirits, who influenced the weather, spreading sunshine or clouds over the landscape, and sending good or bad hunting seasons. They were ruled by an old squaw spirit, said to be their mother. She dwelt on the highest peak of the Catskills, and had charge of the doors of day and night to open and shut them at the proper hour. She hung up the new moons in the skies, and cut up the old ones into stars. In times of drought, if properly propitiated, she would spin light summer clouds out of cobwebs and morning dew, and send them off from the crest of the mountain, flake after flake, like flakes of carded cotton, to float in the air, until, dissolved by the heat of the sun, they would fall in gentle showers, causing the grass to spring, the fruits to ripen, and the corn to grow an inch an hour. If displeased, however, she would brew up clouds black as ink, sitting in the midst of them like a bottle-bellied spider in the midst of its web; and when these clouds broke, woe betide the valleys!

In old times, say the Indian traditions, there was a kind of Manitou or Spirit, who kept about the wildest recesses of the Catskill Mountains, and took a mischievous pleasure in wreaking all kinds of evils and vexations upon the red men. Sometimes he would assume the form of a bear, a panther, or a deer, lead the bewildered hunter a weary chase through tangled forests and among ragged rocks, and then spring off with a loud ho! ho! leaving him aghast on the brink of a beetling precipice or raging torrent.

The favourite abode of this Manitou is still shown. It is a great rock or cliff on the loneliest part of the mountains, and, from the flowering vines which clamber about it, and the wild flowers which abound in its neighbourhood, is known by the name of the Garden Rock. Near the foot of it is a small lake, the haunt of the solitary bittern, with water-snakes basking in the sun on the leaves of the pond-lilies which lie on the surface. This place was held in great awe by the Indians, insomuch that the boldest hunter would not pursue his game within its precincts. Once upon a time, however, a hunter who had lost his way penetrated to the Garden Rock, where he beheld a number of gourds placed in the crotches of trees. One of these he seized and made off with it, but in the hurry of his retreat he let it fall among the rocks, when a great stream gushed forth, which washed him away and swept him down precipices, where he was dashed to pieces, and the stream made its way to the Hudson, and continues to flow to the present day, being the identical stream known by the name of the Kaaters-kill.